The Untold Stories
True Tales Of Temptation
Volume One

True Tales of Temptation

No Part of this book may be produced, stored in a retrieval system, or transmitted by any means without the written permission of the author.

© *2023 Buck Thornton. All Rights Reserved.*

ISBN: 978-1-961392-77-9

Dedication

This work is dedicated to all of the anonymous but very real characters who have entrusted me with their feelings, their fears, their hopes, their love, and their passion.

They have helped me become a student of the game in a very interesting life journey.

I am especially thankful for the support and encouragement that one particular lady provides as I share those experiences. We hope that others can enjoy greater inspiration and passion in their relationship as a result.

Buck Thornton

Table of Contents

Dedication	3
Sweet Torture	5
Flower Bulbs, Stud Horses & Passion	15
The Sisters	31
Hanna's New World	44

Sweet Torture
By Buck Thornton

He had read about Tantric Sex and thought it was an interesting idea; but he doubted if he had the patience or commitment to really enjoy it. On the other hand, he was committed to doing whatever it took to extract the last ounce of pleasure from his partner's body before she went over the proverbial orgasmic cliff. He was sure that Hanna would be a terrific lover because of the very inviting and sensuous phone conversations they had enjoyed, but they had never been together physically and he wanted – no needed - more. He wanted to see if that infatuation and excitement could stoke his passion for years to come.

When he awoke, he felt his normal morning erection and wished that she was there in his bed with him – another day of frustration. Then he remembered that today was special --- it was the day he would actually arrive in her town to spend a couple of days with that sexy lady. He had longed for this day ever since the idea of seeing her after all these years hatched in his brain. They would spend time getting to know one another and building on what they already suspected was a wildfire of passion.

He liked pushing the window during sex, but his overriding rule was that nothing should ever be hurtful, painful or degrading. He enjoyed telling and hearing stories that reflected his fantasies; and he was very much into visual stimulation. That was the key to his very lively imagination. He often got excited when such visuals kick-started his own ideas. Role playing, soft porn and erotic dress-up were things he had enjoyed for their own sake, but they were just tools to make the physical contact between two consenting adults even more heady.

He was a voyeur by nature and he enjoyed watching real people (he and his partner) living out their passion on camera. He knew that most women lacked the confidence to share their fantasies, and he also knew that it took some time to build confidence in sharing secrets comfortably with one another. He did, however, love to see himself and his partner enjoying their bodies to the fullest --- a view that not many couples ever have the confidence to offer as a gift to one another. He had learned that in the right circumstances a camera could be a wonderful way to enhance lovemaking.

As he mused about what might happen that day, he realized that he was approaching her home town. He allowed himself to dwell a minute longer on the possibility of having his fantasies become reality. In a matter of minutes, he would be able to smother that special lady in kisses and let his hugs tell her how much he longed to be with her.

As he carefully followed the directions to her house she waited quietly in her soft, plush bed --- with the front door ajar as she had promised. She spoke softly to him and he followed her voice to her candlelit bedroom where he could smell the incense and see only shadows. He quickly dropped his shirt, shoes and pants at her bedside and she lifted the sheets inviting him to join her in her bed.

They spoke little, but their hands hugged, caressed and fondled each other like they were exploring new and exciting territory. Nothing in the outside world could deter them from the frenzied love making that stretched into the early morning hours. At last, they laid limp in each other's arms after multiple climaxes. As they drifted off to sleep she cooed and wished that he could spoon her every night --- but quickly reminded herself that she just needed to live life to the fullest for the next two days of his visit.

They slept in one another's arms until nearly noon and then spent the afternoon doing household chores, having lunch and sightseeing. There was a lot of unspoken conversation that only their hearts could hear. It was the kind of talk that helped reunite them, and it convinced both that "yes", this was the right thing to do at this moment in time. They laughed about good times, they cried about their losses and they shared their thoughts on a variety of topics. She teased. He teased. But both were careful not to hurt the other because they cherished the bond that was forming between them.

When they returned to her house it was dark outside. She helped him settle in with a glass of wine and suggested that he watch the news while she took care of a few things. He noticed that impish look in her eyes but didn't think anything of it until he heard the bedroom door close and lock. As he sat in front of the TV, he wondered what it was that she was being so private about??? He could hear drawers opening and closing. He heard rustling of bed linens and he heard the water from a brief shower. Other than the low sounds of romantic music, he heard very little for quite some time afterward. He wondered if she had fallen asleep or if she really meant for him to spend the night on the sofa (which would have been fine if that was her preference).

Finally, he heard the click of the door lock and the opening of the door. But before he could look that way, he heard a husky voice command him to look straight ahead. He did as commanded and he soon could smell her perfume and hear the rustle of a night gown or something similar. He also felt the silk of a blindfold against his nose and cheeks plus the warmth and wetness of her tongue in his ear. His member sprang to life immediately, especially when she whispered that he should take her hand and follow her.

He did as he was told and followed his lover to the bedroom. She had ahold of one hand, but with the other he was able to touch the satin of the obviously brief and sexy panties she wore. He could hear the click of her heels on the hardwood floor and her soft giggle as he complied with her every request. The assumption that she was leading him to the bed was quickly proven wrong when she stopped just inside the bedroom door. The door closed firmly and was immediately locked. She instructed him to call her "madam" and made him stand against the bedroom door. He could clearly hear the soft sexy music and smelled her perfume. Somehow, he knew that the room was dark except for the many candles surrounding the bed.

She was leading him with one hand, and he was surprised when she lifted that hand and placed the back of it on the cold surface of the bedroom door. In a matter of seconds, his wrist was secured tightly with a Velcro cuff.

His lover did not allow him the opportunity to say anything because she smothered his lips with warm sensuous kisses that betrayed her excitement and passion. He knew she wanted to be in charge; so even though he tried to question her, she would only put her finger to his lips and tell him to trust her.

She grabbed his other hand and quickly cuffed him to the door with his arms spread wide above his head. If he wasn't completely convinced of her sweet nature, that would have caused some consternation; but he knew that, like him, her objective was to please him, not hurt him! Yet when "madam" pulled one leg back against the door and he felt a cuff encircle his ankle, he began to wonder? The harness that had him secured at three points was obviously one of the things she was preparing while the door to the bedroom was locked.

Then there was quiet. Total quiet.

Finally, he felt her presence near him and felt her wet, warm lips on his. Still she said nothing – just made physical contact so he knew everything was ok. He began to wonder if she was the only other person in the room and he listened hard for any sound that would give him or her away. Instead, all he heard was the opening and closing of a bathroom drawer and the un-screwing of the lid of the massage cream he had bought for their pleasure.

The first body touch he felt was her thumbs on his nipples, and he squirmed involuntarily. His nipples rose to full salute immediately and protruded through his T-shirt; but as quickly as her sexy hands came, they disappeared leaving him longing for more. He also felt the beginning of a pounding erection and the need to squirm to relieve the discomfort. But before he could do much, he felt her hair lightly brushing his neck and face. A few tantalizing strokes and the closeness of her scent made him want to reach out and kiss her.

Next, out of the silence came the feeling of her two hands with fingers spread and moving slowly up his shins and then his thighs --- first on the front and then on the inside of his trigger-ready thighs. He hoped that she would move higher and fondle his manhood; but she stopped discreetly just below his testicles. His erection was so strong that it became painful pushing against his underwear and track suit. He didn't realize it, but a moan escaped him as her hands lingered on his buttocks; and he could feel her breasts as she pushed into him to reach around him. He started to talk but she silenced him and stepped away.

She could tell from his gyrations that he was quickly reaching the point of needing to be set free; but not yet. Instead, she clicked the scissors next to his ear and he stood stock still. He was afraid of what she might do if he had misjudged her and visions raced through his head about her cutting his hair off or mutilating his manhood. Had she not been kissing his neck on the opposite side of where the scissors were, he would have been more afraid; and he could tell from her hot and halting breathing that having him under her control was an aphrodisiac for her. Despite the danger, he could not help but wonder if her panties were becoming wet as she toyed with him.

He was shocked out of his day-dreaming by the feel of her long, sexy fingers playing with his warm up suit draw string. In an instant, she held his balls and manhood in her hand and he could hear her moan as she felt the tool she intended to use so ruthlessly. Other than moaning and squirming, he could do nothing because he knew she held all the cards.

Then he heard the first snip. And then another. He realized that she was holding his stretch pants away from his manhood while she was cutting down the left leg and across his stomach to the right! A few snips up though the draw string and the pants were gone! A few more strokes of the scissors and his underwear also fell away, leaving him standing in front of her with only a very large throbbing erection and a t-shirt. He felt the tease of her warm wet lips on his loins and the heat of her breath as she circled the head of his member with her tongue just once. When he was about to ask her to set him free so he could ravish her body, she withdrew.

When she returned, she made an art form out of touching and teasing his nipples through his t-shirt. Barely touching the ends of them with her forefingers, she would start in the middle and then slowly circle each nipple several times. When he moaned and moved she flicked them quickly but gently with the sides of her thumbs – never letting them return to their soft state. When he next felt her hands, one was holding his shirt away from his body while the other quickly cut the seams of his t-shirt. Then, he felt both of her hands at the top of the T-shirt, each grabbing a fist full of fabric and literally ripping it from his body! The initial shock gave way quickly to a warm sexy feeling that made him realize that he truly was hers to do with as she pleased.

Her breath was coming is short gasps now as she fondled his naked restrained body. He knew that she was close to coming when she ran her tongue over his nipples and traced his stomach down to his crotch. Every time she touched or kissed his nipples he nearly climaxed because the nerve pathways to his penis were unobstructed and running wild with sensations that he had never before allowed himself to enjoy. After all, he was being held hostage and tortured – what could he do? Giving in totally seemed like the right thing to do at the moment, and he absorbed as many of the sensations as possible. There were just too many to identify and they ran together in a flood of emotion and passion that he had never experienced.

Again he was shocked back to reality by another sense – his sense of smell. She kissed him fully on the lips and continued to tongue and kiss his nipples until he thought he could stand it no more. He wondered about her. Was she as turned on being the mistress as he was her slave? The answer came in the form of a sweet womanly scent that he knew had come from her soaking panties and been brushed across his face with her fingers. She stopped and he sucked on her fingers. She was quiet as she withdrew her fingers and he could imagine her using those moistened digits to squeeze her own pretty nipples.

Somehow he knew that she had slipped out of all of her clothes except a bra and panties during one of those quiet spells. He broke the silence by asking if it felt good; and she knew he guessed correctly that she was rubbing the outside of her silk panties with her fingers – and occasionally letting one finger slip inside herself. He could tell by the little gasps she let escape and by the occasional bump of her legs against his. Finally, she spoke; but all she did was to moan "yes" and then her body erupted in a forceful orgasm. He felt it too since she had put one hand on either side of his head and was holding onto the door so she would not collapse. As she shook and trembled, he could feel it through the door; but finally her body went slack and clung to his.

As she regained her strength she turned her attention to him once again. He asked "what can I do to please you Mistress"; and she responded by telling him to just stand there like a good slave for a few minutes more. Those few minutes were bliss as she stroked his member with the massage cream he brought. At the same time she rolled his nipples between her forefinger and thumb – sometimes just standing off to touch them with only a finger while he struggled to get free.

At one point he sensed her dropping to her knees in front of him and kissing her way up his inner thighs and around his testicles. When he was ready for more she seemed to sense it and would tease him with renewed vigor. He begged to be set free, but she would only kiss him in the most sensitive places and whisper fantasy thoughts in his ear. Finally, he could take no more and his body went ramrod straight as the eruption began deep within his balls and shot out onto her stomach and breasts. When spasm after spasm ended, he hung limp in the cuffs and she finally set him free and helped him to the bed where Round Two was about to begin --

The End

The Untold Stories
Book Two

"Flower Bulbs, Studs & Passion"

Flower Bulbs, Stud Horses & Passion
By Buck Thornton

As he sat on the airport bench across from the bottom of the escalator a million thoughts flooded Buck's mind. He arrived early, having carefully maneuvered his knee scooter out of the parking garage and across five lanes of traffic. The honking cabbies and travelers issued a torrent of oaths in 40 different dialects, all of which he assumed wished him Godspeed (or something like that!)

He didn't mind being a little behind the bustling crowd at the Atlanta Airport because he was preoccupied and it had been a while since he'd been mobile due to a broken ankle. He had learned to deal with the limitations the ankle presented, but today he was on a mission – well, really two missions.

The first mission wore on his mind, but it was a necessity. Tomorrow he would again have surgery and he hoped that would "fix" the ankle problem once and for all. The second "mission" took his mind off of the first because it was much more exciting. After weeks of long-distance flirting, he was going to meet a former neighbor he had lusted after for over 25 years.

The infatuation with Sue began in the late 70's when a career move brought him and his family to Chicago. His wife (Ellen) had fallen in love with their new neighborhood. It was a small subdivision surrounding a lake and park. There were lots of kids and plenty of community social events where several attractive young mothers sometimes got emboldened by too much strong drink and risqué conversation ensued. Sue was the most alluring of the forbidden fruit, and she was terrific inspiration for a 35 year-old with an above average sex drive. Sue was a few years younger, tall, blonde and whimsical. She had small but firm breasts but her legs and ass were to die for.

Sue came from a well to do family in the Northshore area of Chicago, and her husband, Rob, was an executive for a Fortune 50 company. He took great interest in people and was somewhat in awe of Buck's western upbringing and rapid career moves. Buck travelled a lot but he had earned promotions in five states before he and Ellen came to Chicago. Rob and Buck became good friends, and Buck quickly found out that they shared a common character trait --- both were horny almost 24/7!

Buck knew that Rob admired – no lusted after – his beautiful wife, and if they hadn't been such good friends, his flirtation with her might have gone farther. Rob was known to grab a quick feel at neighborhood parties after a few scotch & sodas, but Ellen had never told Buck about any such encounter with her. Rob was always very friendly towards her, but that is as far as it went. Of course, there may have been a fear factor as well. Rob had seen the intensity with which Buck played sports and he probably didn't want to trigger any retribution from Buck if he got out of line. Buck towered over him by 5", ran 2 miles a day, played racquetball 4 times a week and grew into 200 pounds of muscle that Rob envied.

Sue was a child of the 60's who went to work as a flight stewardess for United immediately after graduation. She was no stranger to Mary Jane and enjoyed a good party whether on trips or unwinding at home. She openly complained about Rob's shortcomings in the bedroom and there was little else this fun-loving gal would not say.

Even though they had two children, Rob was the caregiver and Sue was the party animal. In those days Buck was almost shy around women, even though there was an X-rated movie running behind his eyeballs whenever he encountered a sexy woman like Sue. He was always polite and "straight" with desirable women, but more than one had sized him up as a case of "still water running deep".

Sue was sensuous – the kind of woman that made you wonder how she would be in bed. He guessed that she was not the sexy quiet type whose every physical pleasure showed on her face. Sue would probably squirm on the bed, tell you every sexy thought she had and take complete control if needed to achieve her orgasm. At least, that is what Buck imagined. When the booze had its effect and the conversation got racy at parties, Sue would give Buck long and meaningful hugs that put physical touch with those sexual musings.

The image that stuck in Buck's mind after not seeing Sue for over twenty years was innocent enough on the surface. It was the only time they had ever actually been alone in over five years as neighbors. It was a beautiful fall day and Buck volunteered to help Sue with a community project. She was the head of the beautification committee and had decided the homeowners association should plant spring bulbs along the tree line surrounding the pond. Buck thrived on manual labor and he couldn't imagine this society gal safely swinging a pick.

Sue had on tight fitting brown slacks that accented her beautiful legs and a low cut blouse that clung to her still firm breasts. Buck busied himself digging holes and planting bulbs (probably upside down) while Sue chattered along. As the sun became more direct and they became more isolated from view, Sue's comments turned to her experiences on her trips and the restraint she had to exhibit to keep from being unfaithful to Rob. As always, she was out in the open about what she wanted and needed from a man --- and was clear that Rob wasn't providing enough of it!

Buck always suspected that Sue considered him a horny, but inexperienced, farm boy who she would love to seduce. Ellen was pretty open with "the girls" after a couple glasses of wine, and Buck suspected she had commented on how insatiable his sex drive was. From Buck's standpoint, this moment in the fall tree line was the opportunity he only imagined. He could imagine their kiss, his hands on her breasts and her grabbing his cock to confirm she wanted it right there in the leaves and right then! He could imagine pulling her slacks and panties off as they fell to the ground just out of sight of any park visitors.

Suddenly they found themselves back in the real world on their knees facing each other less than two feet apart --- with their clothes still on! She saw the gigantic erection through his jeans and smiled a devious little smile. She was used to soliciting that type of reaction with her flirtations, but this time it was different. He wasn't just some half-drunk passenger; he was a sexy neighbor that she had subconsciously fantasized about for a long time.

Buck didn't care if she saw how she affected him, nor was there much he could do to hide it! Part of the reason he was no more embarrassed was that he was totally engrossed in what he saw in her eyes, and he was too busy looking at her erect nipples pushing through her top. Only then did he realize that she was braless. He also was struck by how her perspiration had soaked the blouse so her breasts were defined clearly. Then their eyes met and both knew this was decision point. For a long minute they looked into each other's eyes and sent unspoken messages between them that said "we both want this to happen, but we just can't".

Buck made some feeble excuse and they walked slowly back up the hill giving the autumn breeze a chance to dry her sweat stained blouse and his erection the opportunity to subside.

Shortly after the flower bulb encounter, Buck and his family moved to North Carolina, but he and Ellen remained good friends with Sue and Rob. Because she had free air fare Sue and Rob made several trips to rendezvous with them at various Southeast cities. When they were together on these couples weekends, Buck's imagination of what Sue would be like became more vivid; and she became even more friendly and attentive to him. They both knew what they wanted, the forbidden fruit that neither would cross the line to take.

On one getaway weekend the two couples visited a Kentucky thoroughbred horse farm. A number of racing champions stood "at stud´ at the very upscale ranch where racing enthusiasts would pay to have their mares bred to proven winners. One of the tour options was to see a live breeding session. Both Buck and Ellen had seen horses and cattle mating on their farms out west, but this was something new to Rob and Sue.

The handlers made sure the mare was ovulating and "ready" for the stud. They crowded her into a chute and tied her bridle to allow very limited movement. Then they washed and shaved the area around her vagina. Even a stray pubic hair was a threat to these high dollar encounters. A single seaman sample from a proven winner might sell for up to a half million dollars!

As soon as the stud got close enough to smell the pheromones the mare was emitting, it was "game on" and mother nature took charge. The Vet Tech handling the male horse gave him plenty of bridle rope and as the stud sniffed the female he became increasingly agitated. Eventually, he reared up on his back hooves, moved forward and landed on the mare's back. The amazing thing was that in all of the commotion the stud's penis easily penetrated the mare's vagina on the first try.

Sue was standing near the mare's head and she later commented that the mare's nostrils flared and she spread her back legs so the stud could mount her. I glanced at Sue and could literally see her shorts becoming wet as she watched the stud slide his 24" cock into the now-willing female. His front hooves were tightly squeezing her rib cage and he gently bit her mane as if to say," You are mine". She threw her head back to meet his thrusts and had a look in her eyes that said "Just fuck me!"

When the big male horse climaxed Buck heard an audible gasp escape from Sue's lips. Her nipples were hard, her face flushed and most of her crotch area soaked with her feminine juices. When the big black stallion came he pumped at least a quart of semen into the mare. Much of it ran down her back legs and the smell was unmistakable. When he finished he sniffed her vagina one more time and was led away to regroup for his next "assignment".

After the short but intense event the mare was also turned out into the paddock once she quit shaking. As Buck watched the coupling out of the corner of his eye he noticed a distinct shiver go through Sue's body as the stud came. She had trouble hiding it, but it was obvious that she too had experienced an orgasm watching this primal sex act. Buck always wondered what Sue would have done if he had asked her to meet him in a stall of the barn right then. He did know that Rob reported having the best sex of their married life when they got back to the motel.

Buck was deep into this pleasurable memory and he could feel his member stirring as he waited for Sue to descend the escalator to their designated meeting place in the baggage claim area. He recalled how a twist of luck had brought them back in contact and how quickly things had moved since that occurred.

Buck and Rob made it a point to write a newsy Christmas letter since they had friends scattered across the globe. Rob always made it a point to send a hand written note and Buck would respond. In one of those exchanges Buck learned that Rob and Sue had divorced. Then tragedy hit when Ellen, Buck's wife of 40 years, succumbed to cancer. There were no holiday epistles for a couple years and when he resumed writing them, Buck did not notice that he had not heard from Rob in two years. That was because Rob too had died at about the same time.

Rob's oldest son purchased Rob's condo and he was discarding accumulated mail when he came across the Christmas letter from Buck. He remembered Buck from his childhood so he picked up the phone and brought him up to date on his dad's death. During the conversation, Buck politely asked about his mom, assuming she had married and moved on after divorcing Rob. To his surprise, he learned that she was indeed still single and; in fact, had just ended an on-again, off-again relationship with a retired guy in Wisconsin. He gladly shared her phone number with Buck. Since Buck was recently divorced, he mused that he might just give her a call sometime.

Five minutes after Rob's son hung up, the phone rang and Buck heard Sue's enthusiastic, sexy voice. The whirlwind long distance "catching up" that followed was all green lights and when Buck suggested they meet before his surgery, Sue readily agreed. They had been in daily contact and had even taken an on-line personality profile just for kicks. He had wooed her with a lengthy fairy tale story he had written and talked frankly about how he had concealed his lust for her while married.

Buck had made reservations for connecting rooms at a hotel near the hospital in case one or both needed privacy – or if things did not play out as they hoped. They both knew that they would only have tonight together since his recovery period would be 8-12 weeks. Neither of them could deal with the curiosity and passion they had ignited for 8 more weeks without seeing if there was something real between them.

Buck looked down at his phone one more time to see if she had texted him after landing. Just then he felt warm and trembling hands cover his eyes from behind and felt a warm wet kiss on his neck. "How you doing, Neighbor" were her first words. She had seen him sitting there when she was half way down the escalator and actually ran back to the top so she could take the elevator down and surprise him from behind.

After the initial shock Buck reeled around and hugged Sue with all of his might. Somewhere in the course of his first comments he threw caution to the wind and kissed her deeply. The kiss became an extended French kiss and their embrace seemed to go on forever. Then they heard the approving applause of several bystanders who were apparently touched by this mature reunion! Somewhat embarrassed they proceeded to baggage claim and the parking garage.

The kissing, hugs and conversation seemed so natural as they made it to the parked car. They sat in the car for quite a while just touching and talking; and then they drove to a small Italian café that Buck had discovered on previous visits. Two carafes of wine disappeared in the course of a three hour lunch, and they gradually realized they were the only patrons left in the café.

The conversation had moved from families and old times to the physical relationships of "mature people". Buck was relieved to hear that Sue had a strong sexual appetite as well, and she enthusiastically agreed when he suggested their next stop should be a Victoria's Secret store in the adjacent mall. As they entered the store she invited him to join her in the dressing room --- or at the very least, stay close enough so she could get his approval on various outfits. She made sure he got a number of looks at her in various bras, panties and sexy nighties. After multiple "teasers", she settled on a black lace corset with garters that left about six inches of thigh exposed above the top of the nylons. The low cut corset and black silk panties were plenty to fuel his imagination. He knew tonight would be special.

When the couple finally arrived at the hotel it was late and they both knew they had precious few hours to be alone. The hotel had screwed up and did not have the adjoining room but by now it was obvious that it was not needed! The error did give Sue plenty of ammunition for kidding Buck about his confidence level in being able to seduce her. He made up for it by double checking the reservation for her shuttle ride to the airport since he would need to leave several hours earlier to report to pre-op. Sue was touched by the chivalry and her eyes showed it.

When the door to the room closed, Sue dropped her bag, grabbed Buck by the collar and kissed him hard. She told him to relax, that he had nothing to worry about and that she was delighted to finally be able to sleep with him. He responded by laying her down on the king bed and smothering her with kisses. He loved the little moans and sighs that came from her as his hands cupped her breasts and played along the insides of her thighs. When he started kissing her neck (like she had done his at the airport) she started losing control and reminded him that she still needed to put on a lingerie show for him. He reluctantly let her escape temporarily to the bathroom where he heard the shower running. While she was absent, he added to the ambiance by lighting a couple candles, playing a Neil Diamond CD and spraying a little Code Black on the pillows.

The lights were low and he was already in the bed with only a pair of black silk boxers on when Sue stepped out of the bathroom. In a glance Buck knew he had succeeded in making her feel special. Her attitude was one of sexy anticipation but also appreciation for having the chance to feel like a woman – something he guessed that had been off her radar for quite a while.

Sue struck a sexy pose and Buck responded by picking up his camera and encouraging her to show her stuff. She fully cooperated but Buck had trouble concentrating. Her body showed the effects of six decades, but it was still great. The corset pushed now softer breasts up in a provocative way and the silk panties hugged her hips just fine. After she had showed the camera a number of sexy poses Buck took control and turned her around with her back to him. The black satin blindfold was trimmed in pink lace and shut off all light when he tied it behind her head.

Buck left Sue standing there for what must have seemed like an hour to her. Then he reached around her and for the first time felt those almost naked breasts that he had imagined fondling for so many years. Sue started to speak but Buck whispered in her ear to "hush". She laid her head back on his shoulder and Buck reached up to pull the hair away from her neck before starting to kiss her there. As he did, she seemed to melt into his arms, especially when he reached inside the corset and took one nipple between his thumb and first finger. At the same time he started nibbling on her ear lobe. When his tongue found the inside of her ear, she could stand no more.

Sue turned and found Buck's face with her hands. Seconds later her tongue was searching the inside of his mouth. As his hands slid down her hips he felt his favorite spot – the area inside her thighs where the nylons ended and the panties began. He squeezed her ass cheeks and ran his hand over her smooth panties while she was caressing his neck and chest. When she brushed across his nipples she heard him moan and felt a sudden strengthening in the hard-on he was already sporting. It wasn't long before she reached down and stroked his hard cock through the silk boxers.

It was her turn now. When he started to move she firmly placed one hand in his chest to stop him while the other hand reached for the top of his shorts. Then with one motion she stripped them from him and in a heartbeat her mouth devoured his thick hard cock. She often wondered how well he was hung, and she was certainly not disappointed. Buck had big hands and even those would not fully close around the 7" of manhood that now stood at perfect attention.

Buck did not want to cum too soon because there was so much he wanted to do with Sue, but she was making it difficult to hold out. She knew she had him close when she tasted his salty pre-cum and she begrudgingly rose to her feet when she felt his hands under both armpits.

Sue's feet were captured in sexy black nylons with a seam up the back plus a pair of 3" heels that set off her athletic legs. Right now Buck was interested in getting the shoes and nylons off so he could show her his desire in every way. Carefully he unsnapped the garters holding the nylon tops – first in front and then in the back. With each task he kissed the soft sensuous flesh between the nylons and her panties. He continued kissing down each leg as he carefully rolled the nylons off her toes. With the blindfold in place, she wondered what took him so long. She had felt and tasted his hard cock and was more than ready to have it inside her!

When the second nylon dropped to the floor Buck took her feet and began sucking on each toe. Sue had experienced this once or twice, but never like this! Finally, she blurted out, "Come fuck me". Buck heard the urgency in her voice and knew his duty. He reached into the night stand drawer and ripped open a condom package a smoothly as he could under the circumstances. He wanted to provide protection if she wanted it, but he didn't want to get into a big debate about it at the moment. Sue patiently waited but had a quizzical look on her face. He could see the monologue in her mind "is he doing this because he has a problem or does he think I might have one?"

Once the condom was in place Buck pulled the black silk panties down Sue's legs and used his hands to spread her knees as wide as he could. Even in the dim light he could see the moisture glistening on her pussy lips and when he ran a thumb over the slit it entered her easily. HE COULD SEE THE "WANT TO" IN HER EYES! He moved forward, leaned down, kissed her and with one thrust sent his cock into her hot, wet vagina. She gasped as the thick shaft filled her and he felt her hugging him tightly while enjoying this ultimate intimacy. He responded with an eagerness that caught her off guard. He lunged forward into her again and again like a lineman would hit a blocking dummy. About the third thrust she felt the wetness and knew she had squirted, something that had only happened a time or two in her 60 years. Buck was different than other lovers she had experienced. Her pleasure was more important to him than hers.

After the initial assault he slowed down and played at her opening with his cock --- several slow short strokes followed by one or two deep thrusts. All the time he stared deeply into her eyes and whispered sexy comments that made her feel like the sexiest lady in town. For those few hours she may have been!

Sue was off guard with anticipation and totally absorbed in this passionate encounter. The blindfold was long gone and the corset removed in haste so Buck could suck on her long nipples. She enjoyed her first small orgasm when his mouth was on her breasts and his fingers circled her clit. She was like a hair trigger after that and every time Buck did something different her body responded with greater convulsions and deeper trembling. It pleased Buck greatly when she reached down and removed the condom saying " I want to feel you cum in me". That comment sent him over the edge and cum he did with a loud groan of pleasure and what felt like volume similar to the Kentucky stud's. Sue hugged him closely while he erupted in pleasure and the intensity of his orgasm excited her so much that she too came almost simultaneously.

They collapsed together and held each other while both fell off to sleep for what could have been 20 minutes or two hours. Buck woke first and pulled the sheets up over the beautiful naked blonde lady who had given him so much pleasure. As he shifted she started to wake and he gently kissed her head while his hands caressed her breasts. She nuzzled even closer.

A glance at the clock told him that in less than two hours he would have to leave for the hospital. He suggested a joint shower to make the most of their remaining time. While she was nearly exhausted from the travel and lovemaking Sue readily agreed.

As soon as they were in the shower with the water properly adjusted Buck began lathering Sue's back as well as her breasts tummy and legs, Normally, Sue might have had some misgivings about parading a 60 year –old body in front of a new lover, but Buck's eye contact and gentleness told her she did not have to worry about superficial issues with him. She was completely smitten with him and mused to herself that Buck was the kind of man that a woman waits for when he is at sea. Buck, on the other hand, wanted to make sure that this day with Sue would make her want more. He did.

The reciprocal shower did not last long, partly because of the limited time available, but mainly because Buck needed to experience her one more time. So, after wrapping her hair in a towel and carefully drying the rest of her mature but sexy body Buck spread a dry towel on the bathroom vanity and literally lifted Sue up on it. Her hips were at the front edge with her hands back to support her. Buck spoke not a word. He went down on one knee and began kissing his way from her knee to the natural patch of hair guarding her pleasure pot. He was delighted to see her natural grooming because he always felt it made a woman look more feminine, especially older women.

Sue let a gasp escape when Buck's tongue flicked her clitoris the first time. For a minute he slowly circled her clit with his tongue between sessions of tongue fucking her. After each barrage of probing, he would slow down and even pull back and blow gently to help "reset" her body for another round of licking, sucking and gentle biting. Sue moaned and raised her hips to his kisses, and his expertise brought her a roaring orgasm with several aftershocks. In the end, she sat cross-legged against the full length bathroom mirror and watched as Buck hurried to meet the shuttle to the hospital.

Buck brushed his teeth and was nearly done shaving when Sue crawled off the counter and snuggled up to his back with her naked body. He could feel her nipples on his back and could hear her heavy breathing. She kissed his neck and then reached around him to touch his nipples with both hands. Buck dropped the razor and put his hands on top of hers. She had remembered those special flashpoints that turned him on so much! He stood stock straight and concentrated on the feelings her manipulations were causing. He waited for every contact with the tip of her fingers because there was a direct circuit of pleasure to the head of his penis. Sue watched his cock grow in the mirror, and eventually took his right hand and placed it on his cock. She wanted to see him masturbate!

Buck was surprised but pleased at Sue's "request". He was happy to comply. Within minutes her expert fingers, sexy talk and warm kisses caused him to spray his sperm all over the vanity mirror. His bucking and thrashing were so extreme that he thought he might pass out, but Sue held on until he melted in her embrace.

Buck kissed and tucked Sue back into their bed while he dressed and packed for the 6AM shuttle. He pulled the sheets up over her naked body, kissed her softly on the forehead and gently patted her sweet ass before quietly exiting. The grease pencil message on the bathroom mirror read

"Thank you for making tonight possible. It was wonderful

I promise I will call you as soon as I am able.

I HAVE to see you again - soon! Buck"

The End

The Untold Stories
Book Three

"The Sisters"

The Sisters
By Buck Thornton

Buck Thornton was a busy widower who made time in his schedule for dating pretty older women. He was pushing 70 but very active and most people guessed him at more like 50. He stood six foot tall, and despite a respectable belly, you could still see the remains of the muscular toned college football player in him. His 19" neck and 18" biceps were not gym-generated. They were the result of physical hobbies like landscaping, stone masonry and carpentry. His auburn hair with the silver sideburns showcased a pleasant smile that made it easy for anyone, especially ladies, to talk to him.

A normal day in his independent architectural business was 7 to 7 and he was constantly in conversation with potential clients, current projects owners, contractors, city officials and technical sales people. Buck was a catch and many widows & divorcees were ready to provide both physical and emotional companionship to him.

After his wife's death ten years before Buck had thrown himself into his work in a small town where everyone knew everyone else's business. He continued being involved in community affairs, but he restricted his dating activity to weekends and evenings in two nearby cities where he wasn't known. The "casserole brigade" was frustrated when no local gals seemed able to get Buck's attention. He heard that the rumor mill had written him off because he was "damaged goods", so hurt by the loss of his wife that he could not let himself love again.

As he wheeled into the parking lot of the Destiny Inn, he was glad that he had these short road trips to add spice to his life. Being able to spend time with beautiful, sexy, mature, willing women was something he never anticipated after the unexpected turn of events in his life.

Romance and intimacy were what Buck thrived on. He needed mature conversation and he craved the physical pleasures a man could enjoy in the arms of a woman who was void of hang ups about her body or what was right or wrong. The great losses in his life caused him to be unaccepting of those who failed to realize that all of what they had could vanish in a heartbeat. He had a hard time tolerating "shoulders" (people who spent way too much time telling themselves and others what they <u>should</u> do). Buck had empathy with women who were moving towards that pragmatic approach but weren't quite there yet. He was more than happy to help them see what life could be like on the wild side!

Buck was thankful for internet dating sites that made it possible to identify and communicate with ladies who knew what they wanted and still wanted to live life to the fullest. He had dated women ranging in age from 35 to 74 and he enjoyed getting to know what made them tick and what they wanted. Spoiling a lady was fun, and more times than not they showed their appreciation! There seemed to be no end to the nice women who found themselves on the market at 45 or older, but there were few who wanted to be "grown up teenagers", as Buck described it.

Rachel caught Buck's eye as he was scanning the capsule profiles on a dating site one night. She was over 5'-9", had strawberry blonde hair, a good tan, firm high breasts and legs that never seemed to end. She had taken care of her body and learned the art of attracting a man while growing up on the beaches of California.

Rachel lacked self- confidence despite what she brought to the party, which was considerable. She was the oldest of five sisters and as Buck skillfully peeled back the onion of her background, he learned that there was plenty of real world experience to complement her beauty and sultry personality. He could see that she had a good heart, liked classy things and could be a real fireball when she let her guard down.

Most of all, she was a sexy lady who knew what she wanted!

Rachel had done some modeling and Buck could visualize her in panty hose or lingerie commercials. She liked feeling pretty and enjoyed dressing up for Buck's camera and video sessions. She would dance in her short teddy and modeled provocative bras and panties which she and Buck acquired at Victoria's Secret and specialty shops. Those fashion shows inevitably ended up in a Jacuzzi or bed while the camera recorded their enthusiastic sexual play.

Rachel was basically shy, and strangely enough, so was Buck. His decisive and chatty business demeanor was a persona he developed both for business and social environments. In person, he was honest and direct, but not forthcoming, unless he found someone like Rachel who was a good listener.

Buck believed in getting to know someone in person rather than endless communications by internet or phone. So, Buck invited Rachel for dinner at a family restaurant for their first date. They occupied the quiet corner table for over two hours as they got to know one another.

Rachel arrived at the hostess station of the restaurant looking like a million bucks. Buck hoped that she was the date he was anxiously awaiting, and a broad smile crossed his face when the hostess led her towards his table. With 4" heels, tanned legs and a tight skirt she could have passed for 18 instead of 54 – and it got better the higher Buck's vision rose. Her 38D breasts were contained, but just barely, in a blouse with collar that had no top buttons. It was hard not to stare at the pretty cleavage accented by a single mid-sized string of pearls. She was nervous and glad they had decided to meet in public. But, two seconds after he began to speak in his slow Midwestern drawl, she was convinced he was safe – and more importantly, this was going to be fun! Maybe he was that needle in the haystack she had been seeking.

When she got up for a restroom break, Buck enjoyed watching her tight ass walk away from the table. She suspected he might be watching, so she accented the view with a little wiggle of her voluptuous hips. She stopped just before going down a hallway and looked over her shoulder, as if to make sure he was still there. Her heart skipped a beat when she saw that he was watching her intently, and once she "caught him" he grinned that sexy crooked sweet smile she loved. Damn, he was easy to like! Her panties were already moist when she entered the bathroom stall.

When she returned to the table Rachel slid into the seat next to Buck (instead of across from him as they had been seated during dinner). She was thrilled when he discreetly put his hand first on her knee and then gradually slid it up her thigh under the cover of a napkin. She paused just an instant to ask herself what she was doing letting an almost total stranger feel her up in a public place? The reply was "exactly what I hoped he would do!". That conversation inside her head got pushed aside quickly when his hand made contact with her panties. He was in midsentence commenting that it sure was nice to be able to do the things as an adult that we only wished we could do when we were teens.

After a couple of drinks, the conversation became more provocative and she admitted that it had been "too long" since she had enjoyed the intimate company of a man ---"too long" as in over three years! She was blushing and acted for a while like she was having a hot flash. It was obvious that she had already decided that her dry streak was about to be rained on – and that was just fine with both of them! When Buck asked if she would like to take their conversation to more comfortable surroundings Rachel simply squeezed his hand and smiled. He paid the check and escorted her to his car where she waited until he got a room key for the honeymoon suite at the Destiny Inn.

When she saw the oversized canopy bed and Jacuzzi Rachel let out a squeal and hugged Buck's neck. It was obvious that it had been a while since she was treated to such luxury, and it was hard to control her passion and enthusiasm. When Buck kissed her she concealed neither. Her tongue met his while her hands frantically undressed him. She fumbled with his belt and pushed him down on the bed so she could take off his shoes and socks before sliding his pants down his muscular legs. She then stood up and lay on top of him kissing him madly while she unbuttoned his shirt and began stroking his hairy chest with her hands. She thought that maybe some of her jewelry might have hurt him when her fingers touched a nipple and he let out a groan. She made light of it and said "Here, let me kiss it". She soon found out that the initial groan was one of pleasure, and the more she kissed and touched his nipples the harder his penis got, and the more he squirmed and undulated on the bed. She didn't realize it yet, but the instant she touched his nipples he was her slave. If she had asked him to swim The English Channel at that moment, he would have started looking for his trunks!

Buck knew he had lost the initiative when Rachel kissed his chest, but he made a valiant effort to regain it by slowly undressing her and kissing her everywhere. Her most erogenous zone was revealed when he started nibbling on her ear lobe and kissing her neck. She accused him of tickling her but he knew better. A kiss on her neck was just as explosive to her as fondling his nipples was to him.

Rachel's favorite thing was to have Buck slowly remove her clothes, roll back the sheets, lay her on her stomach and then slowly kiss and touch her body from foot to neck, with special emphasis on her small ass outlined nicely with tan lines. She would moan softly and squirm under his touch, especially when his kisses worshipped her ass checks. In a moment of extreme passion they discovered that his tongue and kisses around her anus were extremely pleasurable. More than once she had pulled away saying "I can't handle it – it's just too sensuous"!

When she was about to reach sensual overload he rolled her over and gently licked her shaven pussy. Her clit was already swollen and easily enraged with a few flicks of his tongue. She responded with a long delayed orgasm that made her nearly faint. When she calmed down he spread her legs and positioned his hard cock at the entrance to her well-lubricated vagina. She felt every inch of his thick cock as it spread first her lips and then her vaginal muscles. She kept encouraging him by commands like "fuck me harder" and "I want you to cum in me". Then she remembered what she learned during foreplay. With both hands at his upper torso she allowed her thumbs to touch his nipples simultaneously. He was already on the verge of coming, but that immediately insured the outcome. He shot a huge load into her as he held her close and whispered "Oh, Baby, you are wonderful".

They both knew that this night was the beginning of something special. They made love every way they had imagined and then slept until nearly dawn. He left after a shower and long, meaningful kissing. Later as she felt the warm water cascading down her breasts and over her somewhat tender pussy, she resolved that there was nothing she would not do to encourage and satisfy this wonderful man who had altered her life.

The Other Sister

Linda was the youngest of five sisters but the closest to Rachel. In fact, they often stayed at each other's apartments and were almost co-parenting a boy that Linda had gotten custody of to protect him from druggie parents. Since neither were married they pooled their resources and struggled financially together.

It was remarkable that Linda and Rachel even spoke to one another. One night in the course of a drinking conversation Rachel revealed that Linda had been the cause of her first divorce. She went on to say that Linda had come to live with them while she finished high school and she had fucked Rachel's husband when she was only 14 years old. Rachel admitted that Linda was extremely well-developed and that her husband lacked any self control. Apparently, he had invited Linda to sit on his lap when they were alone and he took her virginity (without a lot of resistance), according to her sister!

Buck had a vivid imagination and he had difficulty seeing Rachel without mentioning or thinking about the episode between Linda and Rachel's husband. By then the sisters had reconciled and even partied together before Buck came on the scene. He mentioned having a threesome with Linda a couple of times, but it was obvious that Rachel wanted no part of a repeat performance with her man and her sister. Buck had only seen Linda on one occasion when she and Rachel exchanged kids. It was at a motel and Linda had to know why they were meeting Buck there. It was summer and Linda arrived in a bright yellow convertible. Buck introduced himself while Rachel struggled with a car seat.

As Linda shook Buck's hand she looked deeply into to his eyes and smiled a sexy smile. Her meaning was clear. Obviously, Rachel had confided in Linda about Buck's interest in a threesome and now that she had laid eyes on Buck she wanted to make it happen. When Rachel and Buck made love that afternoon they openly fantasized about what it would be like to have Linda join them, and it made their sex even better than ever.

Buck gave the idea of a threesome time to simmer with Linda just to make sure she was all in. When he did bring it up he suggested that Linda would have to pay certain dues to join their little club. Rachel readily agreed because Buck had shown her that he put her first.

Now as Buck parked at The Destiny Inn he was excited to have everything in place before Rachel arrived. They agreed to meet a half hour before Linda was to come. Rachel was right on time and that gave them enough time to strip and jump in the bed for a quickie. As Buck touched Rachel's sweet crotch he could tell that she had been thinking about this too! When he entered her she was so wet that his cock went up to the hilt in one stroke. They fucked hard and he brought Rachel to orgasm before the knock came on the door of room 220. Buck quickly pulled on his pants and shut off the lights while Rachel pulled on her panties and slipped a top over her bare breasts. Then she took up her position behind the door while Buck opened it to a somewhat apprehensive Linda.

Linda's vision was clouded by total room darkness and the bright sunlight behind her. Her first comment was "Is Rachel here?" Her voice was shaking and it was obvious she was afraid that she might be coming into a trap. Then Buck extended a hand and introduced himself in a friendly welcoming manner. At the same time, Rachel stepped from behind the door and gave her a meaningful hug. Rachel then told Linda that she must do whatever she was told and that she would only be allowed to listen to her and Buck making love – and that if she was a good girl she might be invited to join. With that Rachel slipped a black satin blindfold over her eyes and led her over to the desk chair which was placed two feet from the side of the bed.

Before Linda was allowed to sit, she could feel expert fingers at her belt, on her shoes and finally her bra. Rachel and Buck worked quickly to remove all but her panties before making her sit and fold her legs back to the side. When she started to protest having her ankles tied to the chair Rachel reminded her that she needed to submit to their wishes if she wanted to play. She finally began to relax as Buck continued securing her hands and feet. Rachel kept the ball gag hidden behind her back until the last second and then tied the strap at the back of her head. Linda continued to struggle and Buck enjoyed watching her boobs flop from side to side as she did so. This was his first real look at his lover's sister and he was somewhat mesmerized thinking of taking her sexually after her initiation. She had beautiful blue eyes, large well-formed breasts and long blonde hair. The few extra pounds disappeared in her overall beauty.

There was silence as Rachel and Buck moved away from the bed and chair. They let Linda wonder what was next while they quietly kissed and fondled each other. Finally, they removed each other's clothes and moved to the bed. When their lovemaking continued, Rachel was purposely louder and more vocal than normal in order to tantalize Linda. Her moans were punctuated by comments like "Please fuck me" and "Oh, God, yes, suck my clit". As the session wore on, she started begging Buck to cum on her breasts so she could smell his manhood and spread his semen all over her tummy. Buck watched Linda squirm out of the corner of his eye and she was clearly aroused by what she was hearing. When asked if she wanted to see her big sister get bred, she nodded enthusiastically.

When Buck pulled the blindfold and ball gag from Linda's head, the first thing she said was "You son-of-a-bitch!" "Now let me go so I can have fun too". Buck looked at Rachel and she mouthed "NO"! Then she grabbed Buck's hair and guided him to her womanhood where she firmly held his head until she had a loud orgasm. In the meantime, Linda continued to wiggle and tug at the ropes binding her hands. By the time she was free her sister had given Buck a fantastic blow job. When he was at full mast she mounted him in the reverse cowgirl position and was oblivious to Linda's break out.

Buck had seen Linda's escape-in-progress, and he had complete eye contact with her. He gave her the "come hither" sign with his forefinger and seconds later felt her warm, wet pussy descend on his face while she clung to the headboard. He adjusted as quickly as he could and flicked her exposed clit while pushing her forward so her nipples were in full contact with the cold surface of the headboard. In less than a minute she exploded almost in sync with the orgasm her sister was having back-to-back with her.

They created a horny monster in Linda. She wanted to do everything she had listened to and more. When Buck was doing Rachel she would lie next to them and watch Rachel's face during her orgasms.

She was constantly encouraging Buck to cum in her pussy or on her breasts and even on her face. She loved it all!

Buck was very conscious of the fact that these two women were competing for his attention and he tried to spread that attention evenly between them to avoid any jealousy. He felt like a "Buck" during mating season – he literally went from one to the other and fucked or sucked one while the other watched. He didn't have time to become tired and the ladies felt it was their duty to keep him in a constant state of arousal. He was thankful that the little blue pill was producing an erection of envy.

It probably was a byproduct of the "competition" that lead Rachel to whisper in Buck's ear that she wanted to try anal sex with him. Buck didn't say anything but quietly pulled a pillow to the edge of the bed and positioned Rachel so her ass was more exposed to him. While he had participated in anal sex several times he was always hesitant because so many women were afraid of the pain that might be involved with a thicker-than-average cock like his. Nothing was said to the Linda but she focused quickly when Rachel's eyes popped wide open and an audible sigh escaped from her lips. Buck knew that he had entered her secret place because of the surprised but pleased look Rachel gave him. She knew that Linda had real hang ups about anal play because of prior lovers who were not so gentle. Even Rachel was normally not in favor of it, but this felt especially good --- and she told Linda "You don't know what you are missing".

After multiple positions and orgasms the girls and Buck were wearing thin on energy. Buck found himself struggling to maintain an erection after over an hour of constant screwing. It was at this point that Rachel came and stood behind Buck while Linda was getting one more treatment at the edge of the bed. Rachel had laid claim to Buck's load but a sudden massive orgasm overtook him when Rachel reached around Buck and touched both of his nipples. He could feel her naked body against hers and he was enjoying the feel of Linda's natural womanhood while he stroked his cock back to life for one more erection. When he came he let the first spurt land on Linda's belly before rushing to insert his cock in Linda and emptying the rest of his load. Even though he tried to explain to Rachel that he just could not wait any longer, he could tell that her feelings were hurt. It didn't help that Linda was all giggly and made a big deal of having to wash "all that cum" off her body.

Buck, Rachel and Linda were all exhausted after his final explosion. Buck commented to himself that not many men ever get to experience the passion of two mature women who knew what they wanted and could work with each other to get it. He knew there would be more threesomes in their future.

The End

The Untold Stories
Book Four

"Hanna's New World"

Hanna's New World
By: Buck Thornton

Picture Dolly Parton – 5'-2", very small waist, voluptuous hips, nice full breasts, shoulder length blonde hair and a face that captured every man's attention when she entered a room. Hanna wasn't "drop dead beautiful", but her classy look accented everything else. It was hard to describe, but Hanna Hayes had an air about her that made both men and women want to know her – especially men. Buck Thornton was no exception.

Hanna grew up in a town of 20,000 in Appalachia. In addition to being pretty, sexy and friendly, she was smart and a hard worker. Her total commitment to her job was a reflection of her appreciation for the chance to better herself which the large healthcare provider had given her. Even though she had never had the opportunity to go to college, she was promoted from a clerk to department manager. She was professional and polished, and often represented the corporation at trials. She remembered well her early days when she applied for any position in order to prepare for an inevitable separation from her shiftless addicted high school sweetheart.

The first love she thought to be so perfect turned sour immediately. He was 15 years older than Hanna, and he had what he wanted, a 19 year-old trophy bride who everyone wanted to take to bed on first sight. Hanna never knew what it was to make love. She was treated like an owned commodity whose duty was to let him fuck her whenever he wanted. His idea of sex was to pin her small body down to the floor or bed and take what he wanted. It didn't matter to him if Hanna's clothes were torn, a little bruise showed or her young daughter was watching. More often than not he was impotent because of the booze and that made it all worse. He was abusive, both verbally and physically, but she stayed until his drinking, whoring and gambling threatened to destroy everything they had. Her husband's mother gave Hanna the money to hire a divorce attorney.

By the age of 22 Hanna had started over with two children to raise. Her job was her safe haven where she actually got reinforcement and respect, something she had never really known. It was no wonder Hanna distrusted men and was drawn to a circle of women friends. Many of those women, especially the younger wives, came to her for advice and support because they knew she had been through the hammers of hell and came out as a confident, capable career woman.

It was not until Buck Thornton came into her life that Hanna even owned a pair of sneakers. Her normal attire was a classy business suit, heels, nylons and a nice blouse with accenting pearls. How could she know that one of Buck Thornton's hot buttons happened to be women who wore their hair up?

Just as Hanna always dressed like a professional, she was attracted to executives in three piece suits – men of polish and power. She had been propositioned by the best of them and refused them all – all but one who hadn't really asked yet. If he did, her decision would probably have been "yes" provided discretion could be insured. He was married, and she had worked too hard to build a good reputation to be careless. Besides, she only saw him every couple months and she hoped her infatuation with him would pass.

Her breasts were large and firm, and she was used to men only looking at her face after they had their fill of her eye candy. Not only were the breasts about perfect in every other way, but she had pretty nipples that were close to 1/2" long before they were excited. At 54 years old she stood in front of the mirror after her shower every day and remembered the days when her breasts stood firm on their own.

However, she had to admit that her nipples were more sensitive now than they used to be. When she had privacy she would drop the towel and hold her bare breast in her hand, close her eyes and let her fingers roam over it until the pronounced bumps around her nipples were swollen. With her eyes closed she could envision the good sex she had enjoyed with her second husband, Rock.

Rock had been smitten by Hanna, like most men, except that their acquaintance was the result of their church activities. Rock was a great vocalist and Hanna sang in the choir as well. He always made it a point to pay her a lot of attention and complimented her frequently on her singing. Hanna was aware that he was flirting, but she knew he was still married and she was not over the pain of her first marriage. Rock told his golf buddies that he intended to have Hanna for his wife as soon as his pending divorce was over. He did accomplish that, but not until his full court press of over a year finally wore down her resistance.

Hannah refused to have sex with Rock until the honeymoon. She certainly wanted to see what sex would be like with him because their kissing and petting had gotten pretty intense. Many nights before the wedding she left his house with her panties moist from arousal. He appeared to be a gentleman and the complete opposite from her first husband, but she wanted to make sure he wanted her for her, not just sex.

Fortunately, Rock was everything Hanna had hoped for during their courtship. He was tender, patient, kind and horny all the time! She grew to enjoy sex after years of dreading it as a wifely duty. Rock even gave up most of his Saturday morning golf games so he could stay in bed with Hanna all day if she wanted. They loved each other completely but she was feisty and independent. That lead to some pretty vocal arguments, but she could never stay mad at him. For one thing, the make up sex was always sensational!

Hannah was finally whole. She had a wonderful husband, sweet daughters, nice home, almost new car and a job she loved. She still had a little dark side, however. Whenever she could find time she would read sexy novels and watch videos that showed things she knew she would never experience; things like sex with more than one person, seduction of younger men, swinging parties and sex with women.

No one would have ever guessed that Hanna harbored such ideas, but when she did, her masturbation fantasies were intense. Like most middle age women, she had a secret collection of vibrators, dildos and sexy clothing. Sometimes she would come home after work and change into a teddy, slip on silk bikini panties, put on some perfume, lay on her bed and start soft music. Then she would close her eyes and begin touching her nipples and vaginal area until she was ready for something bigger or something that vibrated. She had become very orgasmic and could climax several times an hour with the right stimulation. Sometimes those orgasms were so intense that she would actually pass out for a few minutes. When Rock got home she would be aroused and ready for more.

Then one day he didn't come home. His golf buddies came to the door and she knew something was terribly wrong. He had suffered a massive heart attack on the golf course and never made it to the hospital. Hannah's world imploded once again.

Four years later some of her girlfriends ganged up on her and demanded that she at least consider dating. She reluctantly agreed but told herself she would never again become invested in another man. She just couldn't stand the thought of going through all of this heartache again. She went through the motions but her heart wasn't in it. She began to drink more than she should to overlook the things she didn't like in the men she dated. One guy became kind of a "steady" weekend date and she enjoyed his boat and daughter much more than him. His approach to a great weekend was to begin drinking heavily Friday evening and start sobering up Sunday afternoon. Of course, he was totally in love with her and spent money lavishly to spoil her.

He was NOT the lover of her fantasies, however. His erect penis length was less than three inches, and she could barely feel his presence on a good day, and there were few of those due to his diabetic condition. His 30 year old daughter saw what a mismatch it was and befriended Hannah, much like the numerous young women at work. Being the caring person that she was, Hanna tried to counsel her about not marrying a guy to whom she was engaged. Hanna did not attend the wedding since "stubby" and Hanna were no longer together. She just knew there was no future with him but still cared about his daughter.

Hanna was innocent about other women's interests but she thought it very odd that shortly after the wedding the daughter called and wanted to meet alone "to discuss something very personal". Hanna suspected that she wanted more than just friendship because of the touchy feely approach the girl had always taken with her. She would embrace her and kiss her cheek for the slightest reason, and she was always touching Hannah in places that made Hanna nervous. Hanna liked the attention, but just had never entertained the possibility of being with another woman.

Buck Thorton was one of the few dating profiles Hanna had saved when scanning the website for possible matches in her age range. He was local and his writing and picture seemed professional yet friendly. Besides, there was something about his smile that attracted her. Hannah didn't like wimpy little guys, and even at 60 Buck was anything but that. He was 6 feet tall with a thick neck, big arms and had big strong hands, one of the things that Hanna liked most. In the back of her mind she hoped that all of those wives tales about big hands being a predictor of big cocks was true. No more "stubbies" for her! If she was going to give herself to a man, he needed to be well equipped enough to make her feel him in her.

Buck had been a widower for a couple years, and he had plenty of volunteers to look after his practical and physical needs. He had dated quite a bit out of town for discretion's sake since he owned a couple businesses and was involved in local politics. He had even been mentioned as a candidate for State Representative. Hanna did not know him although he was local and word-of-mouth in small towns was usually pretty effective at match making, especially among older couples.

While she wasn't highly motivated to date at all, Hanna's was curious about this one. They exchanged texts and then a phone call. He seemed a bit nervous and when she finally agreed to meet the only place that came to mind for him was a local doctor's parking lot! She thought that was cute and it gave her the opportunity to drive off if that initial meeting was disappointing. It wasn't.

Buck arrived in his hot red truck a few minutes before Hanna and was actually leaning on the side of the truck when Hanna pulled in. Even from a distance she could tell he was not your typical 60 year-old. He did have a respectable belly, but the rest of him was all muscle. She could not help herself when she snuck a peak at the bulge in his khaki hiking shorts. No stubby here!

She pulled up next to where he was parked, and he flashed a friendly smile as he introduced himself. After a few minutes of small talk he asked if she'd like to go for a ride since it was such a pleasant summer evening. She didn't hesitate because she felt safe – and attracted to him.

As Buck opened Hanna's door and escorted her to his truck he noticed her great tan, shapely legs and a cleavage that took his breath away. He had not envisioned her being so small and feminine! Her loose-fitting summer blouse was beautiful, especially since it was accented by the strand of pearls that lay nicely in her cleavage.

Their first evening together started with a kind of aimless drive that ended at a breathtaking overlook right at sunset. They sat and talked about many things as they watched the lights in the valley come on and the big harvest moon begin to rise. If Buck had planned it this way it would have been great, but to have everything fall in place by coincidence made it incredible! When he helped Hanna into the truck to leave he made quite a production of helping her buckle her seat belt. THAT WAS PLANNED so he could get close enough to kiss her, and she returned his kiss with warmth and encouragement. His comment was simply "wow".

Buck made a mental note to never buy another vehicle with a big console separating the front seats. Had his truck not had one, he was pretty sure this lovely new acquaintance would have scooted over next to him. He had to settle for a warm hand holding the one he offered as he drove toward the doctor's lot where her car was parked. He didn't want to spook her but she had made it clear that she would entertain strong drink on occasion, and Buck asked if she'd like to see where he lived (and maybe have a cocktail).

Hanna probably thought Buck was kidding when he pulled into the 4-car garage at his residence. He wanted her to see that he had means and he was proud of the home that he had greatly expanded just before his wife's death. He knew it was foolish for him to be in a 5,000 square foot house with 7 bedrooms and 6 baths, but it was great for entertaining and he enjoyed cooking for guests. The sunken patio featured a cozy swing next to a flowing waterfall that had absolute privacy. He often invoked his house rule that female summer guests were required to dine topless if he was going to cook for them. It usually worked because wine or mixed drinks typically preceded dinner. He made jest of the topless rule with Hanna because he didn't want to do anything that would cause Hanna to not trust him. She was special, and he wanted her to know that he could be trusted even though their kiss at the overlook told her he was all man.

Buck poured a glass of wine and put some hors devours in the oven because he realized they hadn't eaten anything since they met. The tour took a good while because Hanna had so many questions about the addition and remodeling he had done. She was also intrigued by his very "normal" family, all of whom were professionals with at least a bachelor's degree. She was obviously in awe of those who had been able to further their formal education. He could tell that she loved kids and she wanted to know specifics on all six grandkids. Buck had lived in five major cities and traveled 41 countries of the world, and that experience seemed to strike a chord with Hanna. He really was the professional type that she liked, yet he was laid back and down to earth.

The more they talked the friendlier Hanna became. Buck offered a couple of times to take her back to her car, but she seemed in no hurry to end what had been a wonderful first meeting. They retired to the patio swing for snacks and more wine just as the big moon came over the pine trees that enclosed the sunken patio. This time Buck was more direct about his kiss and they spent long minutes kissing and exploring each other's mouths. He was a good kisser and it was getting to her.

She excused herself for a restroom break so Buck laid his head back on the swing and took in his favorite Neil Diamond song. He was glad that he had wired the speakers into the patio so he could listen to good music while he enjoyed the Great Outdoors. When he heard the patio door open, he saw Hanna outlined in the moonlight holding her blouse in her hand. Her demeanor was playful but extremely sexy as she said that she felt in violation of the house rules and "wanted to get back into compliance". As she came back to the swing Buck's eyes locked on her pretty pink bra and the hourglass figure wearing it. It wasn't like him to be at a loss for words, but he was speechless. He just rose to his feet and kissed her deeply before allowing her to sit in the swing. He loved the way she stroked his face and toyed with his hair while they kissed. She did not pull away when his hand cupped her breast.

After many minutes of kissing and touching Buck slipped out of the swing and knelt down between Hanna's legs. She still had her tailored walking shorts on but it was clear that all she had to do was give him the green light and those shorts would join her blouse on the handles of the swing. He kissed the inside of her knees and the inference was unmistakable. If she let Buck pull those shorts off, he would drive her crazy with his tongue on her clit. He could already smell her womanly scent but he was shocked when she reached behind her and unbuttoned her bra. As she pulled it off her shoulders, he knew she was presenting him with a special gift. Her eyes searched his for approval, appreciation and encouragement. What she saw was awe that this beautiful woman was offering him her most treasured gift. Her breasts were everything he imagined and more. The now erect nipples begged to be kissed and of course he wanted to see and do more!

Buck surprised himself when he asked "are you sure?" As soon as he said it he became alarmed that she may have taken that as a statement that he didn't want to make love to her right there, right now. God knows his erection was about to tear through his shorts, but he didn't want to mess this one up. She was special.

She rose to her feet and answered him "Buck, I have had a wonderful time, and I want you badly, but maybe we should wait". Buck's heart sank until she reached up and kissed him again sensuously. Hanna started to unbutton his shirt and playfully asked "Are you ok with that"? Then she surprised them both when she reached down and squeezed his manhood. An audible sigh escaped her lips and she turned away to grab her bra and blouse. Buck could only say "Maybe you are right to think it over. After all, it's kind of hard to reason with your breasts bare and my cock rock solid!"

When Buck dropped Hanna off at her car, he realized it was almost 1 AM on a work night. He thanked her profusely for meeting him and sharing such a beautiful evening. She said only "I will be in touch". Even one long sexy kiss at her car gave him no consolation. He went home and showered before tumbling into bed naked, but he couldn't sleep. He was tormented by the sight of her breasts, the things she said and the way she reached out for his cock. Not until he grabbed the lube and stroked himself to climax did he fall off to sleep, all the time wondering if she was doing the same thing. She was.

The next day was a busy one but Buck could not help but wonder if he really would hear from Hanna again. He grabbed a quick sandwich and retired to his study with a beer about six o'clock. When the phone rang Hanna's voice was determined and sexy as she said "I want it – I want it all". Buck was stunned but he responded that she should bring her tooth brush and tomorrow's clothes --- and that he would leave a garage door open so she could be more discreet. She liked that, and in 20 minutes he heard her coming into the kitchen from the garage, after closing the big door. She had made the commitment to be alone with this man and show him how much she wanted him.

Their initial embrace spoke volumes for both of them. She was at ease being with him and he was thrilled to have her there. He knew she had not reached her decision lightly and he vowed to do everything possible to reinforce it. There was a quick dinner, wine and quiet time listening to music on the patio swing. When it began to sprinkle Hanna said "Thank God. Now will you take me to your bedroom?" They listened to the soft rain as they made love the rest of the night with the bedroom window open. It was just the two of them in that large beautiful house getting to know each other's bodies every way possible.

It was a muggy night outside so Buck suggested that they take a shower together in his large walk-in shower. He washed her back and then encircled her breasts from behind with his hands while water poured down between them. He couldn't believe how beautiful they were and how it made her squirm with delight as he touched them. She was so small and so feminine that he was afraid to touch her too hard. She didn't share that concern when she turned around and stroked his penis to full attention. Then she dropped to her knees and tongued his cock until he thought he would come. Before he did, he literally picked her up and stood her on the corner bench of the shower. Her natural pussy was just inches from his mouth.

As he licked and sucked at her clit she grabbed for a handhold on the end and side walls. The shampoo bottles went flying but she hardly heard them as her first orgasm with Buck came to pass. She knew it would be the first of many based on his oral skills.

Buck dried her back and blew her hair dry after the shower. They talked about how wonderful her climax had been and she said she wanted to know everything about what it would take for Buck to feel the same intensity. She wanted this to be a mutual satisfaction relationship, especially after she heard how Buck's first wife was somewhat frigid. Bucked loved her dearly and while she had come a long way sexually, she could not have orgasms – possibly because manual stimulation and oral sex were off limits to her. Buck had a high sex drive and he needed someone who shared his level of passion. He finally confided in Hanna that his hot buttons were his nipples, but like many men, he was afraid to share that with lovers for fear they would think he was gay. Hanna's response was to push Buck back against the wall and hold him there while her lips trailed down his chest to his nipples. He was on the verge of orgasm when she released the pressure on his shoulders and he picked her up and took her to the edge of the bed where he devoured her pussy until she shuddered and thrashed around in total bliss. A second climax followed the first and she slapped the bed with flat hands demanding "Fuck me, Fuck me now!" Buck spread her knees, positioned himself at her vagina and did just that!

Hanna was like no one Buck had ever made love to. She was insatiable. Every time she had an orgasm, she would push him away for a few minutes because she was so overstimulated. Then she would kiss him, stroke his cock or kiss his nipples as if to say "OK, let's see how much more pleasure we can find". They slept off and on during the night but every time Buck woke up and looked at this lovely naked creature next to him he would kiss or touch her back to consciousness and then take her in the missionary or spooning position. Her orgasms punctuated the night with loud moans and stifled screams. He was glad they had such privacy so she could release her pleasure vocally.

She was a little grouchy in the morning until she realized where she was and who she was with. When she flashed a sexy smile, Buck imagined her adding the next line "I love you". He could see it in her eyes and he was sure she could see it in his. He came back to the bedroom with coffee and Danish rolls as Hanna was finishing her shower. Buck wanted to take her again right then, but she was late for work.

They talked while she dressed and made plans to go out on Saturday. Both of them needed a rest, but nothing could have kept them apart for long. About 4 PM on Friday the florist delivered a bouquet of flowers to Hanna's office and there was literally almost a cheer from the women (and men) who worked with her. Several mentioned that they knew she had met someone special because she had been smiling so much the past few days (when she didn't have her door closed to catch a quick nap or talk to Buck). She loved it but she was embarrassed. She also knew she could not keep Buck a secret for long. When people learned that they were dating everyone was thrilled.

Buck and Hanna spent every available moment with one another. She would come to his house after work and maybe go home before returning to work the next morning – or maybe not! He rearranged his schedule to include her whenever he made short trips to project sites, and he was sure to always include a nice dinner and a nice motel if possible. On one of those trips, he bought her the first pair of jogging shoes she ever owned so she could tag along on job sites. When they met her daughter for lunch later she asked lovingly" Who are you and what have you done with my mother?" They ate well, drank well and made love like a couple of teenagers. In fact, their sex was better than most people half their age.

Without the concerns of pregnancy, periods, children, reputation or pets, they were free to live life to the fullest. Buck began introducing her to his children and they loved her. His daughter called her "the grandmother we can all agree on". Hanna had Buck over for dinner often and she invited him to join "the girls" (her daughters and her two granddaughters) at an annual Christmas dinner and shopping spree. Hanna broke down in tears of joy when the 8 year-old reached out and took Buck's hand in a crowded store.

Around midnight that night Buck heard the garage door open and her heels click across the hardwood floors towards his bedroom. He turned on the lamp next to the bed to see her dressed in a full length leather coat with fur collar. She had a bottle of wine in her hand and a look in her eye that confirmed why she was there – she needed him to make love to her. Buck slept naked and he had a morning wood erection that got much harder when she opened the coat to reveal a red lacy corset with garters and black nylons. Her only words were "Goddam you, Buck, don't you let me fall in love with you!" His reply was simply "I think that ship has already sailed – for both of us!" They slept little the remainder of the night.

Both Hanna and Buck had vivid imaginations fed by years of written and visual stimuli. There was nothing they would not share with one another – including both actual and imagined events. Her private porn and romance novels led to visions of what sex on the edge would be like. She fantasized about multiple sex partners and being taken against her will by a biker gang. He shared in vivid detail his limited experience at a swinger party, and she was glued to his every word.

One night they talked about escorts and she wondered what their life was really like. She laughed when Buck suggested she might like to "shadow" a good one. After making love she asked if he had ever been with an escort. She was both disappointed and pleased when he admitted to having been with high class ladies a time or two. She was extremely curious and asked a dozen questions. Later they role played with her coming to his room as an escort. He gave her the best oral sex she ever had followed by a hard thrusting fucking that told her he too was turned on by a 3rd person scenario.

At one point Hanna tied Buck's hands to the big sleigh head board and then straddled his face with the command "Eat me!". Each time she climaxed he thought she would be satisfied; but then she would grind her pussy into his face and he would use his tongue to make her explode again. This scenario repeated itself at least eight times until she finally collapsed next to him in a heap of sweating, panting feminine flesh.

The conversation about an escort or a 3rd partner opened the door and their sex was often seasoned with spoken fantasies about hot men and women they saw. They played imaginary games when they were at bars, restaurants or just walking in the mall. In one game, they picked out various couples and then shared their opinions about what their sex life was like.

In another imaginary game, they each got to pick the hottest man or woman in a crowd and explain what turned them on about that person. She (or he) could describe in detail what they would do with that person if they were alone with them for just one hour. Hanna would pick men for her fantasy encounters and Buck got to describe what he would do with the hottest gal if Hanna gave him a hall pass. Hanna would help pick women for Buck's fantasy fucks and she would explain why she thought various gals were hot. One of Hanna's conditions in picking for Buck was that she always got to watch, and that didn't sound all bad to Buck. Both of them had a voyeuristic inclination, and yet it shocked Hanna to think that he would give her the freedom to be with another man as long as _he_ could watch.

The more Hanna heard about Buck's real experiences and fantasies the more she was concerned that he could never be a one-woman man. He assured her that she was all he or any other man needed, but he knew he needed to demonstrate to her that sex with anyone else was just sex, not the love he had for her. The more they talked about non-conventional sex, the hotter their own sex life became.

Buck was a sixty-two year old guy with an abnormally high sex drive, but it took longer for him to cum no matter how exciting the conversation and actions became. He vowed that he would never allow himself to have an orgasm until Hanna had enjoyed at least three. He never had to worry since in one particularly hot session he counted at least 15 such events! He became expert at using his tongue to drive her wild, whether it was circling her exposed clit or thrusting in and out of her swollen pussy. She also loved being on top, especially in the reverse cowgirl position, when his thick 7" cock assaulted the front of her vaginal wall. When she leaned back towards Buck she felt him on her G-spot and she would squirt all over both of them

One night as they were in reverse cowgirl position Hannah leaned forward and grabbed Buck's feet with both hands. Her sweet ass was fully exposed to Buck while his cock was buried to the hilt in her pussy. She was riding her cowboy hard and he let his thumb explore her anus to provide even more stimulation. Hanna came unhinged and started to squeal with passion, especially when he inserted his thumb up to the first knuckle. They had always assumed that he was just too big for such a small gal, but after that night they experimented very successfully with anal sex. She came to enjoy it immensely and he was always gentle so she could.

A favorite pastime on longer road trips was to read profiles of escorts on a website that offered discreet hook ups for upscale swingers. As she always did, Hanna did a quick critique of the escort's body and dress and would make an imaginary rating for Buck to consider. It was becoming obvious that her curiosity about the world's oldest profession was growing, and she became less and less judgmental about those who participated in it – men or women. Finally, on a trip to the beach she suggested that Buck set up a date with one of her "possibles". Buck responded that he would only do that if Hanna made the arrangements. They got into the discussion again about him needing more than one woman, and she acted like it was a deal breaker between them. She made the call and arranged for Buck to meet the #1 choice as soon as they checked into the resort.

Buck still had his doubts about the wisdom of seeing an escort because his lover wanted him to, but she basically bullied him into it. So, he went and he enjoyed the company of a gal who was only "hooking" as a part time job to supplement her income. She was about 30 and pretty down to earth. Her "real job" was being an electrician but she said she liked her escorting side job because she could have sex only when she wanted it, and with only those she selected. She was a nice person with a willing attitude but she could have learned a lot from Hanna on how to please a man. Nevertheless, they played, Buck paid and then headed back to the resort.

The open-minded gal who thought an escort visit was a good idea was obviously pissed when Buck came in. Her suitcase was still unpacked on the bed and she was sitting on the balcony with what was obviously not her first drink. He could tell from twenty feet away that she was an emotional mess. He felt that she had put him in an impossible situation. He was damned if he did and damned if he didn't. When she finally calmed down and quit sobbing, it was obvious that Buck had totally misread Hanna's comments. It wasn't that she didn't want him to visit the escort, she wanted him to take her along so she could watch!

After several drinks and a long talk Buck agreed to make a date with an escort on their way back from the beach. They studied the profiles together, but this time it was Buck who did the qualifying with her on the phone. He was impressed when she insisted on talking to Hanna as well. She explained that she normally didn't entertain couples but added that she felt good about Hanna's honesty regarding her limited (non-existent) experience with threesomes. The gal's name was Janine, and she was both sweet and straightforward. She certainly wasn't going to force Hanna to play with her, but she would welcome it if she wanted to participate. She understood her role as being mainly in showing Buck a good time while Hanna watched.

When they arrived in Janine's town Buck suggested that Hanna call Janine and let her "talk them in" to her place. Janine's place was a refurbished basement apartment in an old but respectable part of town. The main floor apartment was vacant so it was very private. As soon as they pulled into the drive Janine greeted them like long lost friends. The first thing they noticed about her was her genuine friendliness, and the first thing Janine noticed about Buck and Hanna was their classiness. She expected them to be older and less vibrant based on their age, and she was struck by Hanna's beauty. Her comment was "My God, you are beautiful!". Buck was relieved that things had started off so well.

Janine had asked what Buck and Hanna's favorite drinks were earlier, and it was obvious that she had gone out to get the mixers for them. It was early in the evening and they sat and talked in her living room for quite a while. Hanna asked her questions about her profession and seemed in awe of Janine's lifestyle. A new BMW roadster was parked in the drive, and Janine said she had "a very favorable lease" from a local dealer who was a weekly client. She shared some veiled references to high profile clients she saw and at one point said she cleared as much as $ 5,000 per week tax free. She was not what Hanna had thought she'd see in an escort. In fact, it was obvious that Hanna liked her and admired the entrepreneurial spirit she had taken. She was a pretty, friendly young businesswoman who was building a future while providing men (and occasionally, a couple) what they wanted.

Janine came pretty well represented. She was about 5'-4" , pretty, blonde, 30 years old and had the body of someone who worked out 4 times a week. Buck smiled to himself when he considered that her breasts were about the same size as Hanna's but were still firm like Hanna wished. She wore sandals with heels, very short walking shorts and a tight-fitting top that accented those breasts. At one point in the conversation, she obviously got aroused and her long nipples poked proudly through her bra which had firm underwire support but very thin upper cups. It did a very good job of showcasing her breasts and aroused nipples.

Everyone was getting along great and it was obvious that Buck and Hanna were her only date for the evening. She mentioned having her boyfriend come over later but also asked if they wanted to go downtown for dinner since it was Saturday night and there were a lot of groups playing in the old town section. Since they had not eaten the three of them piled into Buck's truck and 15 minutes later, they were sitting at a high-top table in her favorite café. She did not want to drive her new Beamer because it was not yet insured, so she and Hanna squeezed into one seatbelt. As he drove Janine's hand found its way over to Buck's thigh and when that had its desired effect, she began rubbing his crotch. She commented to Hanna that she was a lucky girl and that tonight was going to be fun. Buck noticed that Hanna watched Janine's actions with a big smile and she made no attempt to withdraw when Janine brushed the side of her breast. It was summer, and the two ladies had lots of skin-on-skin contact sharing the front passenger seat. Janine was a pro at keeping Buck interested while warming Hanna up for her first threesome.

The food was good, the drinks flowed and the girls (Hanna and Janine) were chatting a hundred miles an hour. Janine knew everyone in the bar and after Buck left the table for a breath of air she made it a point to introduce Hanna to a number of her guy friends. Most of them were clients and she enjoyed letting them think that Hanna was a new escort that she was trying to help get established. Hanna went along with those introductions and enjoyed the drinks the clients were sending to her. Buck stayed where he could observe them but pretended to be watching a college football game on TV. He had a twinge of jealousy when he saw one of them put his hand on Hanna's thigh, another slyly touch her breast and a third give her a sexy kiss.

Janine knew that all the attention Hanna was getting could be a problem regardless of her curiosity of Janine's lifestyle, so she made a restroom run and laid a big kiss on Buck as she passed. She suggested they leave before things got any hotter, and they walked to the car. Hanna was pretty tipsy and aroused by her imagination of what could have happened if she had really helped Janine with a threesome or foursome.

Buck rearranged things so Hanna and Janine could sit in the backseat while he drove very slowly drove back to her house. Hanna was a chatterbox and she obviously liked the people she met. She did not object when Janine planted Hanna's first girl-girl kiss on her lips. She pulled back a little with a look on her face that said "Wow, that wasn't so bad!". Janine would have kissed her longer and harder if they hadn't just pulled into the driveway.

Both of the girls had plenty to drink but Janine knew it was time to get down to business. She suggested they all take a little nap before her boyfriend, Cliff, joined them. She suggested that Hanna be in the middle of her king bed, with Janine and Buck on each side. Before they lay down, however, she peeled off her blouse, sandals and shorts. She suggested that her guests do the same to keep from wrinkling their clothes. In her excited and foggy state, Hanna readily complied but stopped at her bra and panties. Buck's shirt and shorts were quickly stripped from him by the two women, and he did not object.

Buck found himself faced with two beautiful horny women in their panties. There he stood with a tremendous bulge in his shorts, and it took little urging by Janine for him to remove Hanna's bra, push her bikini panties aside and ram his cock into her. Janine was fascinated by watching these two older lovers make love. Janine was a beautiful woman, but Buck was quick to choose Hanna as the first one to whom he wanted to make love. Janine rolled back from them and whispered encouragement to both of them – things like "That's it, Buck, fuck her. I want to see her cum!"

Hanna was hot and primed. She was enjoying being bred by her man in front of this new friend, and in less than five minutes she was in the throes of orgasm. Buck suspected that Janine was probably pretty good at faked orgasms, and she was in awe of how Hanna reached hers with such genuine total release. Hanna's body went ramrod straight and she began to shudder when that release came. She was very vocal and grabbed Janine's arm at the peak of her passion. Watching her turned Janine on to no end and when Hanna drifted off to recover she whispered in Buck's ear "I need some too, Buck!"

Buck grabbed Janine and pulled her to the edge of the bed where he was preparing to lick her pussy while Hanna recovered. Janine quickly removed her last garment, her panties, and pushed herself up on her elbows ready to receive Buck's tongue and cock. Just then the doorbell rang and she whispered "Oh shit, it's Cliff". When she and Cliff entered the bedroom Buck gave him a firm handshake and welcomed him. Hanna was asleep but he was a little shocked to see that Cliff was maybe 25 years old and very black! Cliff quickly sized up the situation and stripped naked while kissing and caressing Janine's body. His most notable feature was his 10" cock that stood at attention even before Janine began licking and deep throating it.

Buck wondered if Janine had planned this surprise for Hanna or if he really was Janine's lover of the moment. Cliff wasted no time throwing Janine on the bed and forcing his monster cock into her. In her profession she had probably taken some big ones, but it was obvious that his black cock glistening with her juices was hitting bottom on every stroke. But Cliff wasn't paying much attention to Janine. He seemed to be focused on the mature white woman who was now stirring provocatively naked on the bed three feet away. Buck deduced that Janine had invited him over to give Hanna the opportunity to fuck a BBC (big black cock), something that many white women wanted to experience at least once. You could see the wheels in his head turning as he envisioned taking this 60 year-old MILF.

Buck would have been excited to watch Cliff do Hanna if she was in her normal frame of mind. He wondered if she and Janine had arranged this when they were talking on the phone or at the café? Janine looked at Buck, Buck looked at the obviously ready Cliff and all three focused on Hannah. Cliff had pulled out of Janine and moved half way around the bed to position himself for what he knew would be the opportunity of a lifetime to fuck this beautiful old white woman. Buck still searched his eyes and Janine's. He knew they were waiting for his approval since Hanna was still in a fog. At the last minute she looked up at Buck and saw the young black stud with a huge hard on ready to take her. She grabbed Buck's hand, pulled his head to her lips and said "He's black!". Buck motioned Cliff to stand down because he knew that Hanna had once shared with him her hang-ups about interracial sex. He just assumed that she and Janine had discussed the fact that Cliff was black and that Hanna had pushed aside her prejudices in order to experience his unique size.

Janine too was caught off guard by Hanna's rejection of Cliff but she acted quickly by inviting Cliff to do her in the ass instead. Buck apologized to Cliff about Hanna's comment and said he too would like to see him and Janine get it on anally. Cliff turned his attention to Janine's ass and she let out a howl when his monster cock made entry. Meanwhile Hanna had gained full consciousness and she started giving Buck head while she watched Janine "take one for the team". Buck was just entering Hanna when they heard Cliff groan and saw him grab Janine's hips when he exploded inside her ass. Hanna gasped as she saw his load run out of her rectum and down over her vagina before dripping on the sheets.

It had been a long day and Janine invited Hanna and Buck to spend the night at her place before facing the 3 hour drive home. She had sent Cliff away and said all three of them could sleep in her bed. Buck still wanted to do Janine but he decided that Hanna would probably be better off in her own bed. They paid and thanked Janine for a fun time and headed home. Not much was said about Janine or their activity but Buck knew it was on Hanna's mind big time!

A couple weeks went by and Buck guessed that Janine had called Hanna several times. Hanna was obviously still intrigued by Janine's lifestyle but he wasn't sure whether the calls were just girl talk or if

Janine was trying to recruit Hanna for a team performance. Buck let it lie until they were discussing what to do on the weekend. Hanna realized that Buck had not been able to do anything with Janine because she and Cliff had been the center of attention. So, she asked if Buck would like to meet Janine again. Once he determined that Hanna also genuinely wanted to see Janine again he made the arrangements for dinner and a motel. Dinner was very cordial and Buck listened as the girls talked about their hair, nails and friends.

Janine revealed that it was hard for escorts to make friends outside their circle of co-workers because wives and girlfriends were always suspicious of what they might be doing with their men. She seemed to genuinely like and respect Hanna, and she commented a couple times on how Hanna reminded her of her mom. Hanna, on the other hand, went into a motherly mode and started subtly criticizing Janine's drinking and even her slight weight gain.

When they got back to the motel Hanna turned to Buck and said "Ok, it's your turn. Fuck her!" She watched as Buck undressed Janine and ushered her into the bed between the sheets. It didn't seem to bother Hanna when she saw Janine giving Buck a blowjob or when she rolled the condom over his thick penis. One of the conditions Hanna had laid down was that he had to wear a condom if he had intercourse with Janine.

Maybe it was his lover watching that made Buck self-conscious or maybe it was the condom; but Buck had little or no feeling when his cock entered Janine. Here was this beautiful young shapely woman that should have excited him to no end. The only spark he felt was when he kissed her or touched those beautiful natural 38 DD's with the beautiful nipples. Eventually he decided that he would be the photographer and set up the camcorder and camera to make memories of a special game he had discovered.

Buck made these two beauties lie side by side as he applied edible body paint to their faces, breasts and tummies. Then they took turns licking the good tasting material off each other. He started licking Janine's breasts and inner thighs – both of which she enjoyed immensely. Then Hanna made sure all of the paint was off Buck's cock and nipples. He nearly went crazy when both girls sucked at his very sensitive nipples.

He always remembered the look on Hanna's face as she knelt in front of him and Janine. He squeezed the last of the body paint on Hanna's nipples and watched her kneel with clenched eyes as Janine licked it off of the rigid nipples. Hanna had extremely sensitive nipples and Buck could only imagine the determination it took to kneel there and let her new friend slowly lick and suck each point of passion.

Buck could take no more. He threw Hanna back on the bed and drove his cock into her with several hard thrusts. Then he heard Janine saying that she found just a little more of the flavored paint. He withdrew his wet cock and squeezed a line of the paint on Hanna's nether lips. He was about to go down on her before he felt Janine's hand on his shoulder and heard her say "Here, let me". Buck expected Hanna to object, but she lay there with her eyes clenched tightly and her body rigid. She did not object when Janine put slight pressure on her inner thighs and opened her legs to her passionate licking. Buck could not see for sure if Janine was penetrating Hanna with her tongue as she worked slowly to get every last drop of the sweet smelling paste from her vaginal lips. He expected Hanna to object at any minute but instead, Hanna reached out and grabbed Janine's head and pulled it to her pussy, all the time getting more excited.

One of Buck's great regrets was that he gave into passion at that moment and mounted Hanna. He wondered what would have unfolded if he had let these two beautiful women follow their instincts. Buck drove into Hanna time and again with full body contact and his lips kissing Hanna's neck. Hanna had a wild and approving look in her eyes when Back raised himself up on stiff arms. Janine was lying next to her and Hanna reached out, pulled her face down and kissed her deeply.

After a long kiss Janine cupped one of Hanna's breasts and began sucking on her nipple. Anyone passing the door to the room would have thought a virgin was being violated because of the loud moans coming from Hanna. In a way it was a virgin being taken since this was the first time Hanna had ever had another woman.

Buck learned later that Hanna had initiated the lesbian action when the girls took a restroom break. It seemed like they were gone a long time and Janine said that Hanna had thrown her against the door, kissed her deeply, fondled her breasts and rubbed her clit – all like a frantic lover with built up passion. Then they came back to bed to play with the body paint and both just exploded!

As Buck rocked and slammed into Hanna he knew she was close to orgasm so he took Janine's hand and put it between them. Janine's fingers on her clit and Buck's hard cock in her pussy were too much for Hanna. Her explosion drained her and she collapsed into unconsciousness. Janine was concerned but Buck had seen it before when she had unusually powerful orgasms. Buck still needed release so he rolled over and mounted Janine as she lay next to Hanna. She was surprised to say the least but welcomed his insertion. She too was turned on even though she had told them earlier that one real orgasm per night was her max. Buck knew she was honestly enjoying making love the first time to her new lover.

Janine was close to her second explosion of the night when Buck decided to make sure that happened. Just as he slid down her body and tasted her distinct womanly flavor, Hanna came to life and crawled over to Janine. She didn't want to be left behind and she wanted to make sure that her lady lover enjoyed at least the same satisfaction as she had. Buck had moved back up and was attacking Janine's pussy. They kissed and Hanna fondled her bare breast while her other hand caressed her tummy and lower body. Janine did indeed reach her second orgasm of the night just as Buck exploded in her. All three of them fell asleep in each other's arms.

Two weeks went by and not much was said by either Buck or Hanna about the bi-sexual events of their last date with Janine. Buck often found Hanna day dreaming, and he was pretty sure he knew why. Hanna was having a hard time not dwelling on the feeling of Janine's hands, lips and beautiful body. She wondered if her first lesbian experience was really as good as she remembered? Hanna had let something slip and Buck was sure that Janine had called Hanna and invited her to come over for shopping, sex and lunch. He never knew for sure whether Hanna accepted that invitation, but it was obvious that Janine wanted to pursue a relationship with Hanna – and he was 90% sure that feeling went both ways. The roadblock was Hanna's need to acknowledge her lust for the feel of another woman.

Buck had a plan when he called Janine to arrange a Friday night date, which also happened to be his birthday. Hanna pressed him as to what he wanted for his birthday but Buck's only reply was to that he wanted Hanna to dress in her little black cocktail dress, heels, nylons and pearls. Hanna thought it was a long way to go for dinner, but it was his birthday, so she did what he asked --- and she looked like a million bucks! She did not know that Buck had arranged a surprise for Hanna and Janine. He deflected Hanna's questions about where they were going until they were close to the motel where they were to meet Janine. Buck finally explained that what he wanted for his birthday was for Janine and Hanna to be alone together so they could make love with privacy. Hanna started to object but started warming to the idea, "Is that is what you really want?". Buck replied that he only wanted the best for Hanna even if it meant sharing her with someone else on occasion. Hanna had tears of joy in her eyes as they sat in the parking lot and prepared to meet her lover. Janine had done her part to prepare by getting the Jacuzzi suite at the Hilton. She had the right music, candles and lingerie to seduce any woman. When she came to the door the lights were low and the music soft; but the best thing was Janine all dressed in a long negligee cut high on her hips and held together between her breasts with a spaghetti tie string.

Hanna clutched Buck's hand tightly as they walked down the hall to room 360 at The Hilton. When Janine opened the door Buck caught the smell of Janine's perfume. He disengaged from Hanna and gave Janine a long deep kiss. At the end of it he mouthed "thank you" then turned to Hanna. She gave him a long passionate kiss and said "Happy Birthday Darling". Then Buck took her hand and placed it in Janine's. His only instructions were to call him when they had enjoyed all that they could with each other. He said he'd be at the mall next door or the Hilton bar. It was about 7:30.

Buck was tortured by what might be going on with the two women he thought were the sexiest in the world right then. He was hoping in particular that Hanna would have the opportunity (and inclination) to perform oral sex on Janine since he was sure that was an experience she had never had. During her first experience with Janine, Hanna had been the receiver, but he hoped they would have the time, privacy and inclination to expand on that.

It turned out that Hanna took full advantage of her hall pass. As soon as they were alone Hanna became the alpha female and stripped Janine's clothes from her in a frenzy. She then ordered her to lie down and kissed her body from toe to top. Before Hanna went down on her she spent a long time kissing her mouth and rubbing her now naked nipples across Janine's. The sensation was tremendous, and by the time Hanna's tongue touched Janine's clit she was ready to explode. Janine then showed Hanna the joys of "scissoring" and "humping" on Janine's thigh. Finally, they called Buck about 9:30 just before they jumped into the shower.

When Buck knocked on the door Hanna greeted him with a huge smile, big kiss and a hug that showed her appreciation for his allowing her to be with Janine alone. Buck recognized the unique smell of Janine's scent when he kissed Hanna, and he knew that she had "gone all the way" with her. He started to ask what had happened but Hanna drug him by the hand to the edge of the bed and said "Let's make love".

Hanna had tasted sex with another girl and enjoyed it. But she knew in the end that she preferred her man when she really wanted to feel like a woman. Buck was glad to be the one she wanted.

The End